Pirate Hank's
Plank

by Penny Dolan and
Nacho Gomez

W
FRANKLIN WATTS
LONDON•SYDNEY

Franklin Watts

First published in Great Britain in 2016 by
The Watts Publishing Group

Text © Penny Dolan 2016
Illustrations © Nacho Gomez 2016

Series Editor: Jackie Hamley
Series Advisor: Catherine Glavina
Series Designer: Peter Scoulding

A CIP catalogue record for this book is available
from the British Library.

ISBN 978 1 4451 4581 5 (hbk)
ISBN 978 1 4451 4579 2 (pbk)
ISBN 978 1 4451 4580 8 (library ebook)

Printed in China

FSC
www.fsc.org
MIX
Paper from
responsible sources
FSC® C104740

Franklin Watts
An imprint of
Hachette Children's Group
Part of The Watts Publishing Group
Carmelite House
50 Victoria Embankment
London EC4Y 0DZ

An Hachette UK company.
www.hachette.co.uk

www.franklinwatts.co.uk

The sea was calm and
the sky was blue.

Suddenly, Joe heard a
loud shout.

"Over there! A ship!"
called Spy-Eye Sam.

At first, everyone was
excited.

The strange ship drew
closer and closer.

8

Then they saw the flag.
"It's a pirate ship!" shouted
old Captain Cod-Face.

9

Too late! The band of
pirates leaped aboard.

The crew feared for their lives.

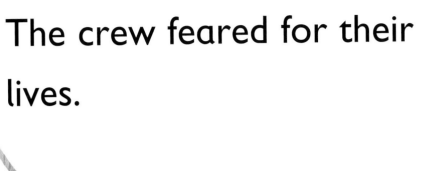

The pirate chief boarded the ship. He walked around the deck, sword in hand.

13

"I am Hard-Nose Hank.
Beware this plank!"

15

Everyone looked at the plank, and at the deep, deep sea.

Nobody wanted to walk the plank.

"Who will go first?" asked Hank, smiling his mean pirate smile.

He put his boot on a big barrel. Nobody spoke.

Joe thought. He looked hard into Hank's eyes. "I will," he said, stepping forward.

"Now?" said Hank,
grinning. "Really?"
"Yes. I've got a great idea,"
said Joe. "Just watch."

Joe put the plank across
the barrel.

"Sit on that end," he said, and Hard-Nose Hank did.

"This is great!" Hank shouted. "Thanks!"

They played see-saw for
hours.

Then they played swinging from the rigging and all sorts of games ...

... until it was time to sail away again.

a

b

c

d

e

f

Put these pictures in the correct order.
Now tell the story in your own words.
Can you think of a different ending?

excited   scared

terrified

happy   thrilled

worried

Choose the words which best describe Captain Cod-Face at the beginning and end of the story. Can you think of any more?

Answers

Puzzle 1

The correct order is:

1e, 2a, 3b, 4f, 5d, 6c

Puzzle 2

Beginning   The correct words are scared, terrified.

The incorrect word is excited.

End   The correct words are happy, thrilled.

The incorrect word is worried.

Look out for more stories:

Bill's Silly Hat
ISBN 978 1 4451 1617 4

Little Joe's Boat Race
ISBN 978 0 7496 9467 8

Little Joe's Horse Race
ISBN 978 1 4451 1619 8

Felix, Puss in Boots
ISBN 978 1 4451 1621 1

Cheeky Monkey's Big Race
ISBN 978 1 4451 1618 1

The Animals' Football Cup
ISBN 978 0 7496 9477 7

The Animals' Football Camp
ISBN 978 1 4451 1616 7

The Animals' Football Final
ISBN 978 1 4451 3879 4

That Noise!
ISBN 978 0 7496 9479 1

The Frog Prince and the Kitten
ISBN 978 1 4451 1620 4

Gerald's Busy Day
ISBN 978 1 4451 3939 5

Dani's Dinosaur
ISBN 978 1 4451 3945 6

The Cowboy Kid
ISBN 978 1 4451 3949 4

Robbie's Robot
ISBN 978 1 4451 3953 1

The Green Machines
ISBN 978 1 4451 3957 9

For details of all our titles go to: www.franklinwatts.co.uk